CAT CHARACTERS – A to Z

Published by American Editions
Copyright © 1995 by American Education Publishing
No part of this book may be reproduced in any form
without written permission from the publisher.

Published by agreement with FORLAGET APOSTROF,
Copenhagen, Denmark
Originally published as KATTENES ABC

Printed in China

Illustrations copyright © 1993 Mimi Vang Olsen,
545 Hudson Street, New York, NY 10014

English text copyright © 1995 Tracey E. Dils

ISBN 1-56189-398-6

CAT CHARACTERS – A to Z

Illustrations by Mimi Vang Olsen
Text by Tracey E. Dils

AMERICAN EDITIONS

A a

Every cat that you meet, every kitten you see
Has its own special place in this cats ABC.
They may be tiny or thin or a little too round
White, gray, or spotted, orange, striped, or brown.

But each of these cats needs a name of its own
A name that is perfect for that cat alone.
So join us and consider each of their names,
And follow along in this alphabet game.

Abbie our "A" puss is part acrobat.
From cartwheels to flips, she's a most limber cat.
And when she is finished, she fluffs up her fur
And ends her routine with a slow, steady purr.

©Mimi Vang Olsen

B b

While you have been busy at school all day,
The cat you call Ben has had plenty to say.
At ten, he meowed from under your bed.
By noon, he was purring in the sun on the ledge.

While you were at recess, he yowled at the door.
By three, he was snoring from this spot on the floor.
And that's where you found him, all curled on the rug,
Awaiting your greeting and soft, tender hug.

© Mimi Vang Olsen

C c

For Claire and Cassandra, there's nothing so fine
As a warm summer day for a carrousel ride.
High on jeweled saddles they ride up and then down,
While proud painted ponies spin them round and around.

When the ponies have stopped and the ride is complete,
They'll leap to the ground on their soft padded feet.
The two slink away, their heads in a spin,
Yet they can't wait to go on this ride once again.

D d

"There's nothing to do," Daphne mews with a sigh
To her sister named Debra who lies by her side.
"All we do every day is stretch, lounge, or sit,
I tell you I'm getting quite tired of it!"

"Hush, sister," purrs Debra. "You must learn to relax.
We've got food, fresh water, pillows for our backs.
And if sometimes you find life a bit of a bore
Just sleep on it dear—then do it some more!"

© Mimi Vang Olsen

E e

Even elegant cats like Edgar and Em
Need to venture outside to explore now and then.
Between bushes and trees, they'll creep and they'll crawl
And then settle right down in this place by the wall.

They'll circle the spot and then bat at the air,
A strange thing to do because nothing is there.
On leafy brown beds, they'll stretch out for a rest
And sleep the day through, nature's most pampered guests.

F f

Felicia's been busy grooming her fur.
Little Felix spent his day learning to purr.
Frederick has been prowling about since noon,
Exploring each corner, checking each room.

But when their day's over and their work is done,
They'll curl up together, mother, father, and son.
And share a warm hug as they lie down to rest.
Cuddling, after all, is what families do best.

Mimi Vang Olsen.

G g

Gertrude and Grace aren't the only ones dressed
In white, orange, and black, their calico best.
Meet their best friend, George, who has come for a visit.
Is he a cat? A mouse? Please tell me, which is it?

He doesn't purr or meow or act like a cat.
He can't be a mouse, his middle's too fat.
Perhaps he's a gerbil, but he seems kind of big.
Oh, I know the answer—he's a plump guinea pig.

imi Vang Olsen

H h

The tide's going out and the wind's from the west,
These are the conditions ships' cats like the best.
So Hannah and Horatio have climbed on the bow
Of their sturdy gray houseboat and with a meow,

They'll shove off from shore and head 'cross the bay.
With the wind in their faces, their fur damp with spray,
They'll sail off to sea for adventures more grand
Than any they'd find if they'd stayed on dry land.

© Mimi Vang Olsen

I i

She has cushions and pillows on her custom-made bed
But Isabelle likes this old basket instead.
It may not be soft or silky inside,
But it's just the right place for a kitty to hide.

Inside its straw sides, she's hidden from view
Until she decides to play cat peek-a-boo.
So close both your eyes and ask, "Who is that?"
Then open them and say, "It's my favorite cat!"

Mimi Vang Olsen

J j

Jeremy and Jessica have set themselves right down
On a quilt of bright blue that's been spread on the ground.
From these soft cotton seats they'll see spring's finest show.
They'll watch each bud blossom, each blade of grass grow.

They'll see each new flower, they'll explore every bloom.
They'll breathe in the sweet air, spring's finest perfume.
They'll listen for bird songs, the bee's slightest hum.
They'll know all this means the new season's come.

K k

Kait was a strong, nimble cat in her day,
But now she's grown older, her hair has turned gray.
Her eyes have gone cloudy, her belly is thick.
Her meow is much softer, she's not nearly as quick.

But even though some things have changed for old Kait
And she seems to prefer life a bit more sedate,
She is still at your side, now just as then,
Your gentle companion, your best ever friend.

L l

The studio's closed, the artist's gone home
And Laura and Lucy are left there alone.
These two crafty cats will both do their part
To turn blank canvas into works of fine art.

They won't waste a minute, they'll get busy creating
A sculpture, collage, an impressionist painting.
When they're all finished, they'll clean up their supplies
And leave for the artist their artful surprise.

© Mimi Vang Olsen

M m

They have five tiny toy mice and a spider to track
But that's not enough for Molly and Mac.
They need a new playmate, the human variety
To enliven their formal feline society.

Cats need real people as well as stuffed toys
To play games and cuddle, that's what they enjoy.
So give them fake creatures and fill a small zoo
But remember, your cat's best plaything is you.

©Mimi Vang Olsen

N n

When night falls, you hear the door open and creak
And you know your cat Nancy has decided to sneak
Out into the garden to explore the blue night,
Her cat eyes aglow in the moon's faintest light.

You think she might sit among the spring flowers
Or prowl the stone walkways through night's darkest hours.
At dawn as you're waking she'll mew to come in
And you'll never quite know just where she has been.

Mimi Vang Olsen

O o

Ollie and Ozzie have a place that they share,
A red and gray cushion on a brown wicker chair.
They meet there each day to discuss all the news
The latest in fashion, their political views,

The weather, the arts, what's in and what's out,
There's not much that these friends won't gossip about.
They're entitled to their thoughts, to share them quite proudly,
But must they discuss their opinions so loudly?

P p

Six Persians live in this plush penthouse flat.
The striped one's named Percy, the black one's called Pat.
There's Penelope, Pia, Pedro, and Paul.
And then there is Peggy who's not a real cat at all.

You see, pampered Peggy is a little confused.
Don't tell her the truth--she won't be amused.
So let's keep her secret since her cat friends don't mind
That she's living her life as a kitty canine.

©Mimi Vang Olsen

Q q

Quint's not the type to wander or roam.
He much prefers life closer to home.
While other cats may seek riches and treasure,
Quint is quite happy with life's simpler pleasures.

He finds that his family's old patchwork quilts
Are softer by far than China's best silks.
Some well-worn old toys, his master's tweed hat
Are treasures enough for this homey cat.

R r

Roberta, Rebecca, and their friend Renee
Have decided to meet in the garden today.
They'll meet in a special spot in the shade
Of rhododendron flowers and leaves of deep jade.

Rebecca will call the meeting to order.
Roberta will act as the day's note recorder.
Renee has refreshments and when they've finished that,
They'll all settle down for a post-meeting nap.

Imu Vang Olsen

S s

When the winter has put on its coat of pure white,
And the wind's icy fingers take hold of the night,
Like polar explorers, Sarah and Sam
Head out to discover the barren wasteland.

They'll fluff up their fur against the air's chill
And hike 'cross the frozen valley and hill.
And when it's too cold to walk anymore,
They'll hold up a paw and scratch at your door.

Mimi Vang Olsen

T t

Tina, Theresa, Tam, Tai, and Tess
Are hiding in a place their father won't guess.
Between the folds of this colorful curtain
They'll never be found, these cats are quite certain.

But their father knows well how to play hide and seek
And he takes just a minute, one quick little peek.
Now his kittens have learned what all children know:
Your father will find you wherever you go.

Mimi Vang Olsen

U u

Ursula really wants to be good.
She tries to behave, to do what she should.
But behaving's not easy for a curious creature,
Finding mischief to make is her natural feature.

And so when she curled up in this old bag of yarn,
She really didn't plan to do any harm.
But once she climbed in there, she just couldn't stop.
Now she's tied all this yarn in a tangle of knots.

© Mimi Vang Olsen

V v

Vera is telling another tall tale
Of dogs that can float and cats that can sail
Along on the clouds high up in the sky.
She insists she has proof, cats really can fly.

Neither Vianna nor Vincent have ever quite seen
A cat in the clouds or a dog on the wing.
And Veronica and Van are skeptical too.
But Vera's not worried, she knows that it's true.

Mimi Vang Olsen

W w

For their holiday, Will and Wendy escape
To enjoy the beauty of a different landscape.
The gentle green slopes, the forest of trees,
The wind's quiet sigh, the fresh alpine breeze.

Quaint villages that boast fairy tale towers,
The gentle sweet odor of blue alpine flowers.
The mountains, the lakes, the icy cool streams,
Are the stuff that make up their vacation dreams.

Mimi Vang Olsen

X x

Xandra and Xavier don't mean to boast
Of their lovely new villa on the Mexican coast.
With a garden, a spa, and a fancy guest suite,
It's the perfect place for a feline retreat.

For cats, there's a room of a special design
With tunnels to crawl through and ladders to climb,
Some catnip to chew on, a few old toy mice,
This villa is simply a cat's paradise.

©Mimi Vang Olsen

Y y

When dinner is ready and you sit down to eat
Yolanda and Yanni will sit by your feet.
Or jump on the table to try something new
A taste of your salad, a bite of your stew.

But cat food is really the best kind of feast
For even the most demanding of beasts.
They may howl and meow and act rather rude
But cats really should nibble their own special food.

Z z

These two gorgeous cats spend most every day
Among the fine art on this antique buffet.
There's a blue willow platter, some rare Chinese vases,
Exotic art objects from faraway places.

But far more valuable than any of that
Are the snapshots displayed of four special cats.
These are their nephews, and soon they'll be back
To visit their Aunt Zara and their dear Uncle Zack.

We've named all these cats from A clear to Z.
We've considered their traits, what kind they might be.
And so we have finished our cat alphabet
But wait just a minute! We're not done quite yet.

We have a few felines who still don't have names
So let's keep on playing our cat-naming game.
Now it is your turn to get into the act
And decide what to call this marmalade cat.

©Mimi Vang Olsen

And here's a white one who is perched in a chair
What would you call her if you found her there?
Look in her eyes and study her face,
Consider her manner, her style, and her grace.

And then choose a name that suits only her.
You might call her Julie or just Jennifer.
She could be named Kristen, Carmen, or Candi,
She might be a Katherine, or maybe a Sandy.

And now we've come to the last cat in our book
What would you call her? Have a good look.
She has eyes of deep amber, a coat of light gray
And she seems to have something important to say.

Now comes the most important cat-naming part
Of this ABC game, it's really an art.
To choose a name for your own feline pet,
You just think through your own cat alphabet.

And if you still need a name for your cat
Ask your cat what she thinks about this name or that.
She'll meow or she'll purr and you'll know she agrees
That you've found her a place in the Cat's ABCs.

Mimi Vang Olsen